We are the Dino Diggers – the best in Dino-Town.
We put things right when they go wrong and never let you down.

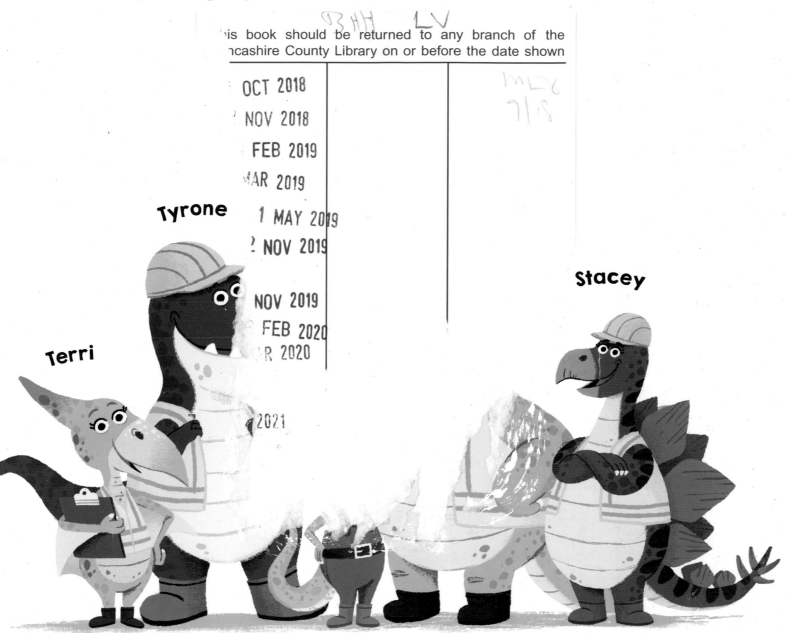

Tyrone

Terri

Stacey

For Reuben – R.I.
For Dad – C.C.

Bloomsbury Publishing, London, Oxford, New York, New Delhi and Sydney

First published in Great Britain in 2017 by Bloomsbury Publishing Plc
50 Bedford Square, London WC1B 3DP

www.bloomsbury.com

BLOOMSBURY is a registered trademark of Bloomsbury Publishing Plc

Text copyright © Rose Impey 2017
Illustrations copyright © Chris Chatterton 2017

The moral rights of the author and illustrator have been asserted

A CIP catalogue record of this book is available from the British Library

ISBN 978 1 4088 7244 4

All papers used by Bloomsbury Publishing are natural, recyclable products made
from wood grown in well managed forests. The manufacturing processes conform
to the environmental regulations of the country of origin

Printed in China by Leo Paper Products, Heshan, Guangdong

1 3 5 7 9 10 8 6 4 2

DINO DIGGERS

Digger Disaster

Rose Impey   Chris Chatterton

BLOOMSBURY

LONDON OXFORD NEW YORK NEW DELHI SYDNEY

Today Tyrone T. rex and the Dino Diggers are building a new car factory for Mr Ali O'Saurus.

But Mr Ali O'Saurus doesn't look very happy.

He's a busy man. And an impatient one.

"I can't wait till the next Ice Age," he tells Terri Dactyl.

"I want those foundations laid by the end of the day."

Terri's the one in charge. "Leave it to us," she says. "You know our motto."

The Best in Town –
Dino Diggers
Never Let You Down

Terri hurries to get on with the work but a sudden wind almost blows her plans away.

Luckily, Ricky Raptor, the new apprentice, is there to catch them. Well almost . . .

The other Dino Diggers laugh as they watch
Ricky chase the plans.

Once he's caught them, Terri tells Ricky to
hold on to them. "That's your job for today.
Back to work, the rest of you," she squawks.

Tyrone T. rex is ready to start digging out the foundations.

And Stacey Stegosaurus is ready to move the earth.

"You know what to do," Terri tells them. "Keep an eye on the plan and work as fast as you can!"

Yes, Boss.

As usual, Tyrone's in such a hurry to get started he barely looks at the plans. "Fast?!" he boasts, "I'll be like a mighty meteorite. You watch me!"

In no time Tyrone and his backhoe have dug a huge hole and Stacey has soon cleared away the earth. But suddenly . . .

BANG!

. . . everyone is wet through and it isn't even raining! The water seems to be coming out of the ground. Uh, oh!!
The backhoe has cracked a water main. Water gushes everywhere like a great waterfall.

CRASH!

All the Dino Diggers come running. "Someone get that water turned off!" squawks Terri.

Bruno Brachiosaurus goes off to do it, but Tyrone thinks fast, too.

He cleverly turns the backhoe bucket to cover the hole and the water stops gushing – for now at least.

"What a Dino-Digging disaster!" groans Terri.

Terri can't understand how this happened – that water pipe was clearly marked on the plans. How could Tyrone have missed it?

Uh, oh. Now Terri can see what's happened. Someone has turned the plans upside down.

"Sorry, Boss," says Ricky, blushing.

Terri shakes her head and looks at the clock.

How will they ever be ready for Mr Ali O'Saurus?

"Leave it to us, Boss," says Tyrone.

The Dino Diggers are soon working super fast to put things right.

Once the water's properly turned off, Tyrone quickly clears the soil from around the pipe,

while Stacey speedily clears it out of the way. "We're both working like mighty meteorites," she laughs.

And so is Bruno. As soon as the pipe's clear,
he expertly swings his tall tower crane into action.
First, he carefully lifts out the broken pipe . . .

then gently lowers in the new one.

All day the Dino Diggers work hard to lay the foundations for the new car factory.

Terri's very proud of them all.
"What Dino-Digging teamwork!" she says.

When Mr Ali O'Saurus comes back on
site he looks much happier, too.
"I knew I could rely on you," he tells Terri.
"The Dino Diggers never let you down!"

Hooray for the Dino Diggers, another job well done!
Here are other stories full of Dino-Digging fun.

Digger Disaster

Crane Calamity

Dumper Truck Danger